FRECKLEFACE STR🍓WBERRY
Backpacks!

For kids who have backpacks
—J.M.

Text copyright © 2015 by Julianne Moore
Jacket art and interior illustrations copyright © 2015 by LeUyen Pham

Visit us on the Web! randomhousekids.com

Educators and librarians, for a variety of teaching tools, visit us at RHTeachersLibrarians.com

Library of Congress Cataloging-in-Publication Data
Moore, Julianne.
Freckleface Strawberry : backpacks! / Julianne Moore ; illustrated by LeUyen Pham.
pages cm. — (Step into reading. Step 2)
Summary: "Freckleface Strawberry and Windy Pants Patrick make messes in their backpacks."
—Provided by publisher.
ISBN 978-0-385-39195-5 (trade) — ISBN 978-0-375-97367-3 (lib. bdg.) —
ISBN 978-0-385-39194-8 (pbk.) — ISBN 978-0-385-39196-2 (ebook)
[1. Best friends—Fiction. 2. Friendship—Fiction. 3. Backpacks—Fiction. 4. Orderliness—Fiction.
5. Schools—Fiction.] I. Pham, LeUyen, illustrator. II. Title. III. Title: Backpacks!
PZ7.M78635Frd 2015
[E]—dc23
2014040654

MANUFACTURED IN MALAYSIA

10 9 8 7 6 5 4 3 2 1

FRECKLEFACE STR🍓WBERRY
Backpacks!

by Julianne Moore
illustrated by LeUyen Pham

Doubleday Books for Young Readers

Chapter 1

Freckleface Strawberry
loves to go to school.
When she goes to school,
she brings her backpack.

Her backpack
has bugs on it.
Freckleface Strawberry
loves bugs.
In her backpack, she has

1. pencils

2. homework

3. gum

Windy Pants Patrick
loves to go to school.
When he goes to school,
he brings his backpack.

His backpack
has dogs on it.
Windy Pants Patrick
loves dogs.
In his backpack, he has

1. pencils

2. homework

3. a donut

Freckleface Strawberry's
mom and dad
did not know
Freckleface put gum
in her backpack.

Windy Pants Patrick's
moms did not know
Windy Pants put
a donut in his backpack.

They gave their children
a big kiss and said,
"Have a great day
at school, honey!"

Freckleface Strawberry
and Windy Pants Patrick
went to school.

Chapter 2

At school,
children sit
at their desks.

12

At school,
children open
their backpacks.

At school,
children hand in
their homework.

All the children had
the same homework.
They had colored in
their maps.

Almost all the children's
maps looked the same.
They were colored
and flat.

Freckleface Strawberry
looked at her homework.
Gum was on
her homework.

Windy Pants Patrick
looked at his homework.
A donut was on
his homework.

Freckleface Strawberry's
homework was colored
but not flat.
It had a big lump of
gum on it.

Windy Pants Patrick's homework was colored but not flat.
It had a big lump of donut on it.
Uh-oh.

Chapter 3

"Time to hand in
your homework!"
the teacher said.

Freckleface Strawberry
and Windy Pants Patrick
did not know what to do.
So they handed in
their homework.

"Look," said the teacher.
"Freckleface Strawberry
and Windy Pants Patrick
have something extra
on their homework."

"Their maps are not flat,"
said the teacher.
"Their maps have mountains.
Good job.
You both worked
extra hard."

Freckleface Strawberry
and Windy Pants Patrick
knew they had not
worked extra hard.

They looked at each other.
"We have to tell her,"
they said.

Chapter 4

After school, Freckleface
and Windy Pants
talked to the teacher.

"We are sorry," they said.
"We did not mean
to make mountains.
We put gum and a donut
in our backpacks.
We made a mess."

"That is not a mess,"
the teacher said.
"That is only a mistake,
and sometimes we learn
lessons from mistakes.
Like how to make
mountains.
Or not to bring gum and
donuts to school."
And then she smiled.

Chapter 5

The next day,
Freckleface Strawberry
and Windy Pants Patrick
went to school.

In their backpacks,
they had

1. pencils

2. homework

Oh, and

3. bugs

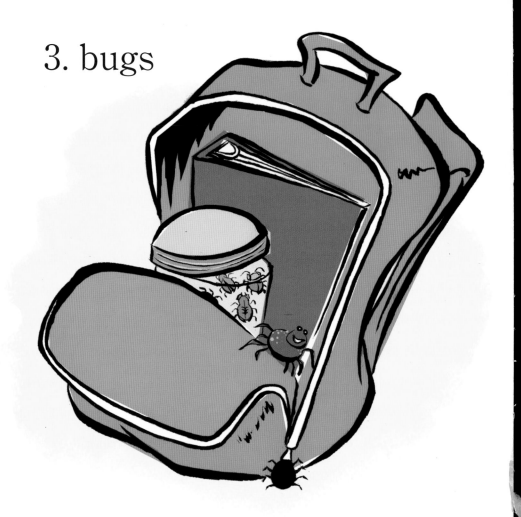

Freckleface Strawberry
loves bugs.